Shadow in the Woods
and Other Scary Stories

Read more MISTER SHIVERS books!

MISTER SHIVERS

Shadow in the Woods
and Other Scary Stories

WRITTEN BY
MAX BRALLIER

ILLUSTRATED BY
LETIZIA RUBEGNI

ACORN™

SCHOLASTIC INC.

For Ollie and Evie, the coolest brother and sister duo around. –MB

I want to say thank you to my family for being my biggest support
and always believing in me. –LR

Special thanks to Jenny Palmer for her contributions to this book.

Library of Congress Cataloging-in-Publication Data

Names: Brallier, Max, author. | Rubegni, Letizia, illustrator.
Title: Shadow in the woods and other scary stories / written by Max
Brallier ; illustrated by Letizia Rubegni.
Description: First edition. | New York : Acorn/Scholastic Inc., 2020. |
Series: Mister Shivers; 2 | Audience: Ages 5–7. | Audience: Grades K–1. |
Summary: Hugh does not like walking home alone through the woods which
the other children say is inhabited by a monster, but today he has no
choice, and it is not only his shadow that follows him—and that is only
one of five scary stories included in this collection.
Identifiers: LCCN 2019029369 (print) | LCCN 2019029370 (ebook) |
ISBN 9781338615418 (paperback) | ISBN 9781338615425 (library binding) |
ISBN 9781338615432 (ebk)
Subjects: LCSH: Horror tales. | Monsters—Juvenile fiction. | Children's
stories, American. | CYAC: Horror stories. | Monsters—Fiction. | Short
stories. | LCGFT: Horror fiction.
Classification: LCC PZ7.B7356 Sh 2020 (print) | LCC PZ7.B7356 (ebook) |
DDC 813.6 [Fic]—dc23
LC record available at https://lccn.loc.gov/2019029369
LC ebook record available at https://lccn.loc.gov/2019029370

10 9 8 7 6 5 4 3 2 1   20 21 22 23 24

Printed in China   62
First edition, July 2020
Edited by Katie Carella
Book design by Maria Mercado

TABLE OF CONTENTS

Dear Reader,

I like scary stories with strange shadows and spooky sounds— just like the stories in this book.

An odd box was left on my doorstep last night. A rusty padlock for a school locker sat beside it. Here is what I found inside:

- An owl feather.
- A flashlight battery.
- Fingernail clippings.
- A tuft of red hair.

There was also a notebook in the box. This note was taped to it:

PROMISE ME, MR. SHIVERS, THAT YOU WILL SHARE THE STORIES INSIDE THIS BOOK.

Long ago, I learned to keep my promises. So here I share those strange and scary stories. But be warned, they might make you shiver.

Mister Shivers

SHADOW IN THE WOODS

Hugh hates walking through
the woods in the dark.

But it's the only way home
from school.

Older kids say a monster lives
in the woods.

"The monster is big, with fangs,"
the kids say.

"The monster calls out your name,"
the kids say.

"When you hear your name—RUN!"
the kids say.

Hugh usually walks home with a friend. But today Hugh stayed late at school.

So he is alone.

Hugh walks quickly.
Sticks snap.
Leaves crunch.

Hugh hears these noises every time he walks home.

Then Hugh hears a new noise: **"Hoo!"**

Hugh knows it is an owl hooting.

But Hugh feels like somebody
is following him.

He looks behind him. Nobody is there.

The moon is full. It's so bright that it casts long shadows.

"Hoo!" Hugh hears the owl again.

Hugh still has the feeling he is being followed. He stops and listens.

Quiet. Only—

"Hoo!"

Hugh is almost to the clearing.
He can see the old barn ahead.

Hugh's shadow is long. He remembers,
"The monster is big, with fangs."

"Hoo!"

He remembers, "The monster calls out
your name."

Hugh walks faster. He says, "I am not a scaredy-cat."

"Hoo!"

As Hugh passes the old barn,
his shadow rises from the ground.
He sees it on the barn wall.

Hugh **stops**. But his shadow
keeps moving.

The shadow turns toward him.
Its huge mouth opens.
The mouth is full of fangs.

Suddenly Hugh understands.
This is **not** his shadow.

There is **no owl** hooting,
"Hoo!"

It is the monster in the woods,
calling his name, **"Hugh!"**

He remembers the warning: "When
you hear your name—RUN!"

Finally, Hugh starts to run.
But it is too late.

THE MONSTER IN MY ROOM

Ruby was **sure** a monster lived under her bed.

She could smell the monster.
It stank like the inside of
a wet garbage can.

Sometimes she could even
hear it growl.

Ruby's older brother crawled
under her bed.

"There is no monster here,"
he told her.

But Ruby was **sure** a monster
lived under her bed.

Ruby's dad pushed boxes
under her bed.

"Now there is nowhere for a monster
to hide," he told her.

But Ruby was **still sure** a monster
lived under her bed.

"The monster only comes out in
the dark," Ruby told her family.
"That is why you can't see it!"

But **no one** believed her.

Ruby's brother gave her a flashlight.
"Use this when you feel scared,"
he told her.

That night, Ruby climbed into bed.

Suddenly she heard a noise.

Oh no.

Ruby turned on the flashlight.

She saw a shadow on the floor.
It came from **under the bed**.

Ruby wanted to call out for help.
But she was too scared
to open her mouth.

She dropped the flashlight.
THUMP! It fell to the floor.

That's when she saw **the hand**! A large, hairy, purple hand! Eight long fingers were wrapped around the flashlight.

Ruby could not move.

The hand came toward her. Closer and closer. Then—

"Hey, kid," the monster said. "You dropped this."

FINGERNAILS

"Stop that!" Tommy's grandmother told him.

Tommy dropped his fingers from his mouth.

"Please stop chewing your
fingernails," his grandmother
begged him.

Tommy looked at his left hand.
The nail of his pinkie finger was
a little crooked.
His thumbnail was jagged.

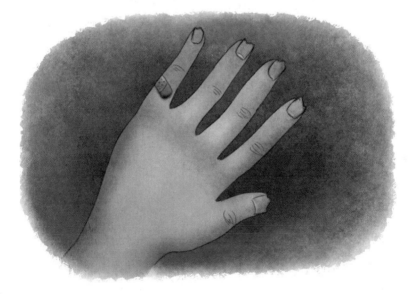

"**Your** fingernails are so dirty!
Look at how perfect **mine** are,"
Tommy's grandmother said.

She frowned. "Promise me that you
will never chew your fingernails
again."

Tommy looked at his grandmother's nicely shaped nails. They were boring. Too clean! Too neat!

He liked his own short, jagged nails much better.

Tommy nodded. "I promise I will never chew **my** fingernails again," he said.

"Good!" His grandmother smiled.

She leaned back in her chair
and closed her eyes. She fell asleep.

A bit later, she felt something strange.
It felt **warm** and **wet** and **gummy**.

She also heard a strange sound.
It was a tiny **crunching** sound.

Tommy's grandmother opened
her eyes.

Bits of fingernail were littered
across her lap.

Tommy stared up at her as he chewed and chewed and chewed...

THE WRITING ON THE WALL

Sophie's mother parked the car.
"Welcome to our new home, Sophie!"

The house looked even worse than
Sophie had imagined.

Its roof drooped. A loose shutter slapped in the wind.

"I don't want to live in this old house," said Sophie.

"You're going to love it." Her mother smiled.

Sophie walked inside.
The floors creaked.

"It's creepy in here. I feel like I'm
being watched," she said. "I want to
go home."

"This **is** home," her mother said.

Sophie climbed the dusty stairs. The steps moaned.

She pushed on the door to her new bedroom. The door did not move.

"This house doesn't want me here," Sophie thought.

She pushed harder.

Finally, the door opened.

The room was cold.

She opened the curtains.
Beetles escaped.
The window was cracked.

A chill ran through Sophie.
She hoped it was only the wind
coming in through the glass.

"I don't want to live in this house,"
she said.

SLAM! The door closed behind her.

Sophie spun around.
Somebody was there!

But it was only an old mirror.

"I don't like it here," she said through clenched teeth.

It was getting dark.

Sophie's bed would come tomorrow.
So she unrolled her sleeping bag.
The floor was hard. There was
dirt everywhere.

"I don't want to sleep in this house!"
Sophie said.

Her mother called upstairs. Her voice
was cheerful. "Good night! Sweet
dreams!"

Sophie ripped open her backpack
and grabbed her red marker.

She wrote on the wall:

When Sophie woke in the morning,
the red marker was gone. Instead,
a black marker lay on the floor.

And written on the wall
were the words:

THE ANIMAL
BEHIND THE LOCKER

Emma set her books on the floor
in front of her locker. School was over.

Then she heard the noise.

SCRATCH-SCRATCH.

She looked in the locker.

SCRATCH-SCRATCH.

She reached in to grab her backpack.

"I think there's an animal
behind my locker!" Emma said.

SCRATCH-SCRATCH.

Emma heard the noise again.

The janitor came by.

"Some poor animal is trapped
behind my locker!" Emma told him.

He listened carefully.

"I don't hear anything,"
the janitor said.

Soon, the hall was empty.
Emma shut her locker and turned to
walk away. Just then—**CLICK!**

The lights went out.

"I **know** there's an animal trapped behind my locker!" Emma said. "I **need** to set it free."

She took a deep breath and opened her locker.

She squeezed all the way inside.

The locker's back was loose.

She pushed and pushed and—**POP!**

Emma was now **behind** the locker.

Then—**CLANG!** The locker's back snapped into place.

Emma was trapped.

It was dark. Just a bit of light
snuck in.

SCRATCH-SCRATCH.

But this time it wasn't a noise.
Something rough was **scratching**
her cheek.

Emma blinked. It was hard to see.

SCRATCH-SCRATCH.

This time the scratches hurt.

Then Emma saw it.

A huge spider was hanging beside her.
It had long, hairy legs.

The spider smiled at Emma.
Sharp, wet fangs stuck out.

Emma tried to move. But she was caught in the spider's sticky web.

Her feet were glued to the gooey ground. She reached for the cold, metal locker . . .

SCRATCH-SCRATCH.

This time, Emma was the one scratching.

Emma was the animal trapped behind the locker!

ABOUT THE CREATORS

MAX BRALLIER is the *New York Times* and *USA Today* bestselling author of more than thirty books including The Last Kids on Earth series, the Eerie Elementary series, and the Galactic Hot Dogs series. Max lives in New York with his wife and daughter.

LETIZIA RUBEGNI is a children's book illustrator. At an early age, she fell in love with storytelling through pictures. She carries her red sketch pad everywhere she goes to capture any interesting ideas. She lives in Tuscany, Italy.

YOU CAN DRAW A SPIDER!

1. Draw a big circle for the spider's head.

2. Add a half-circle for the first part of the spider's body.

3. Add the second part of the body and put two feelers on the head.

4. Draw six eyes on the head.

5. Add two fangs with four tiny teeth in between. Then draw eight hairy legs.

6. Color in your drawing!

WHAT'S YOUR STORY?

Emma finds a spider behind her locker.
This book ends with Emma trapped there.
Imagine what happens next.
Do **you** think Emma gets away?
Write and draw your own scary story!